All global publishing rights are held by
Ukiyoto Publishing

Published in 2024

Content Copyright © Kajari Guha
Artist: SRAC

ISBN 9789362690852

All rights reserved.
No part of this publication may be reproduced, transmitted, or stored in a retrieval system, in any form by any means, electronic, mechanical, photocopying, recording or otherwise, without the prior permission of the publisher.

The moral rights of the author have been asserted.

This is a work of fiction. Names, characters, businesses, places, events, locales, and incidents are either the products of the author's imagination or used in a fictitious manner. Any resemblance to actual persons, living or dead, or actual events is purely coincidental.

This book is sold subject to the condition that it shall not by way of trade or otherwise, be lent, resold, hired out or otherwise circulated, without the publisher's prior consent, in any form of binding or cover other than that in which it is published.

www.ukiyoto.com

Then the daily chores like brushing teeth, taking bath, drinking milk were carried on with Mom's help.

Next with the arrival of the yellow school bus and Papa's hug and kiss, the day started.

At noon, she was back home.
Sona Aunty was there at the bus-stop.

Then the story began, she listened to it with eyes wide open and gulped the food. Next it was time to take rest. She lay on her bed with the baby panda while Sona Aunty caressed her forehead, continuing the story. Rosie closed her eyes and found herself taking a stroll on the beach. She met Pink, the long legged flamingo and Rick, the rooster.

Rosie closed her eyes and found herself taking a stroll on the beach. She met Pink, the long legged flamingo and Rick, the rooster.

Suddenly Pip, the silver scaled catfish waved her fins constantly and popped up. The blue ocean water dazzled with her slender silver body.

Pip invited Rick to sit on her back. Rick had a tank tied around his leg that is known as Scuba, a Self Contained Underwater Breathing Apparatus.

Pink an expert scuba diver, asked Rosie to sit on his back. Rosie also had the same tank on her back so that she could breathe easily. She felt gaga about the sport exploring the lakes, rivers, quarries, kelp forests and coral reefs. Pink dived with his long legs with artificial fins attached to them and spread his wings, as if soaring in the sky. Rosie had to wear a dry suit to stay warm.

Pink suggested shore diving to Bonaire, the Caribbean island while Pip suggested muck diving at Dumaguete and Dauine coastline. Pink and Rick agreed and followed Pip.

Rosie loved the house reefs and vibrant mandarin fish. The sea beds, sea grass ,octopuses, frogfish, pipefish and cuttlefish were wonderful! Rosie felt charmed with the pink, black, white and tiny yellow clown frogfish. They inhabited the reefs with beautiful ghost pipefish and flamboyant cuttlefish. Next they moved towards the calm and quiet village of Anilao, the capital of the Philippines, a paradise for macro photography.

Then they headed towards the Cayman Islands. The dive sites were very close to the shore. They visited the legendary Bloody Bay Wall and Turtle reef. The water temperature was 78 to 82 degrees Fahrenheit there, so Rosie wore a wetsuit to protect herself from the heat. Their final goal was Malpelo Island. All four of them got surrounded by the silky sharks.

Rosie went to the bathroom, washed her face and changed her dress. Sona Aunty helped her out.
They all got settled in the car with the picnic basket and reached their destination within fifteen minutes.

Mamma, Papa and Sona Aunty stared at her and she danced like Pink, the flamingo. The sun set to rise again the next day. Rosie too left for home with Mamma, Papa and Aunty, charged with fresh energy for the following morning.